For ANNE INGRAM
without whose help many
books would not grow

COLLINS PUBLISHERS AUSTRALIA

First published in 1986 by William Collins Pty Ltd,
55 Clarence Street, Sydney NSW 2000
First published in paperback 1988
Reprinted 1989

Text copyright: © Hazel Edwards 1986
Illustrations copyright: © Rod Clement 1986

Typeset by Savage Type Pty Ltd, Brisbane
Produced by Mandarin Offset in Hong Kong

National Library of Australia
Cataloguing-in-Publication data:

Edwards, Hazel, 1945 –
Snail mail.

ISBN 0 7322 7206 8
1. Snails – Juvenile fiction. I. Clement, Rod.
II. Title.
A823.3

SNAIL MAIL

Hazel Edwards   Illustrated by Rod Clement

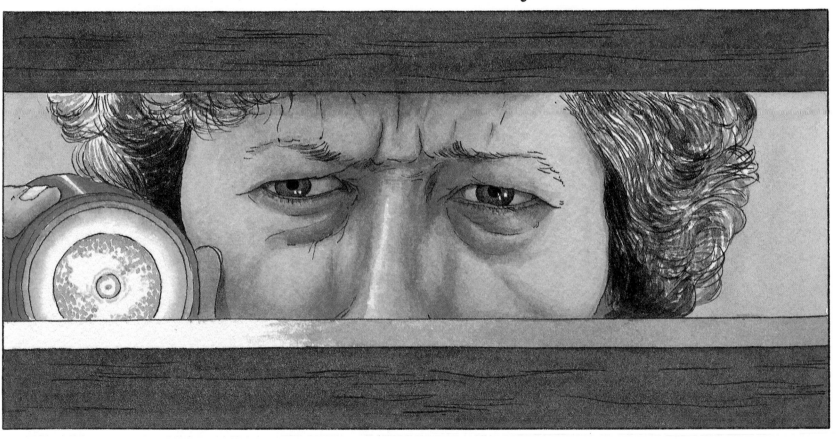

Collins
Publishers
Australia

Today *they* are sad because *that* letter didn't come.
Only three postcards, two bills and a paper
arrived with a THUD!
I know everything.
I'm the snail who eats the mail.

Garden-years ago, I did ordinary snailish things.
Like munching mint, chomping chives and tasting tomatoes.
Most run-of-the-garden snails don't read a lot.
But read-eating is fun.
I'm the snail who ate all the herb labels.
Now *they* don't know which is which.

Unfortunately, my second cousins, twice removed,
ate *her* prize lettuce.

"I'll spray those snails!" *she* cried.

"No." *He* was still a snail lover. "Don't pollute our world
with sprays."

So I slithered away from the garden school.
Now I'm the snail who eats the mail.

From here I can see my 'Meals on Wheels' arriving.
The mailman pants up the hill to Number 28.

Through the slot comes a three course meal.
Envelopes of different sizes, ideas and flavours.

Thirty-three cent stamp is 'Flavour of the Month'.
I'm the snail who digests the mail.

But I'm a gourmet snail, eating only a little of the best.
I'm the snail who even enjoys overseas mail.
In three different languages.

Each morning, as the sun's rays
shine through my slot,
I do snail-aerobics.
Especially, my eye exercises.

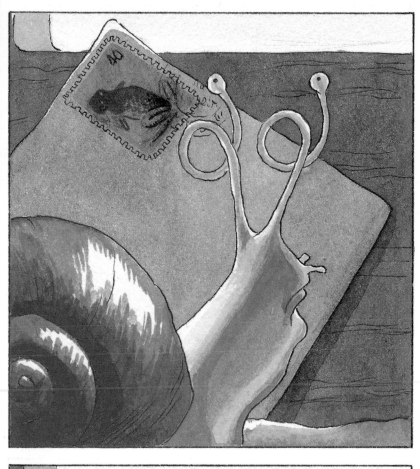

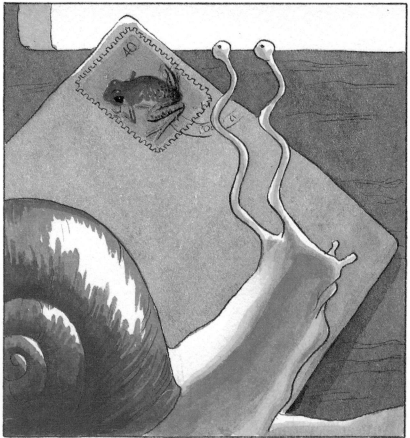
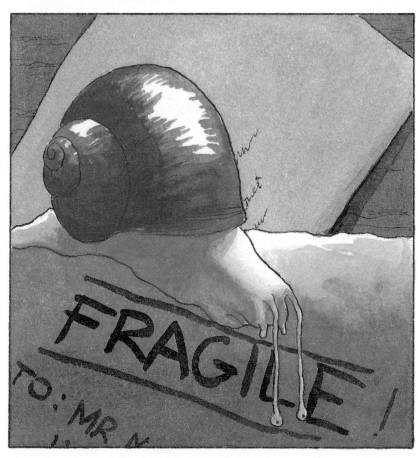

On Monday, a 'Froth-a-Lot' shampoo sample
was dropped inside my mailbox.
Eating that was a mistake.
I didn't read the instructions.
Now I'm the snail who froths a lot.

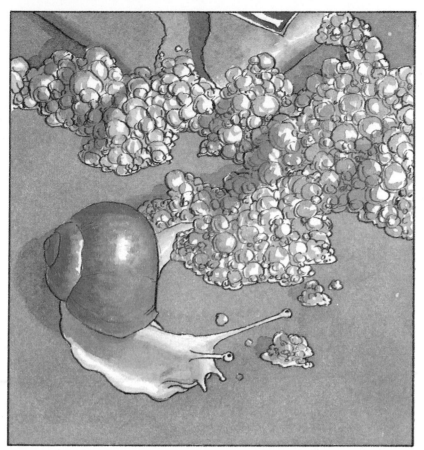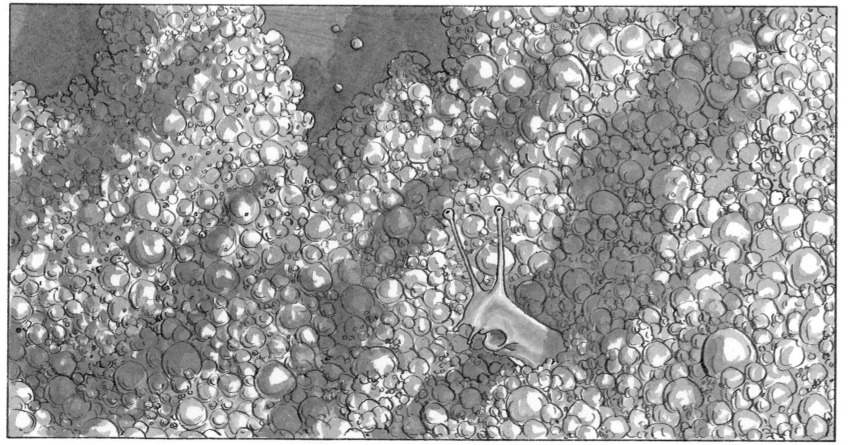

Catalogues used to be my favourite snack food.
On Tuesday, *she* put a NO JUNK MAIL PLEASE sticker
just below my slot.
Now I'm the snail who's on a diet.

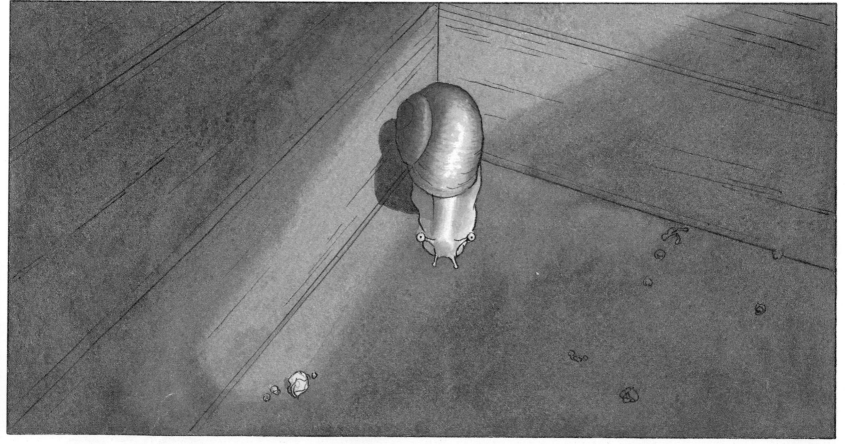

On Wednesday, I nibbled just the cover
of her 'Food' magazine.
Even with the back door closed,
I could hear *her* complaining.

He warned me, through the slot,
"In French restaurants, people EAT snails."

Thursday, *she* tried to find me, with a torch.
Luckily, the mailbox is extra deep and dark.

"I'll stamp on that snail!   If I can find it."

"Live and let live," *he* said soothingly.

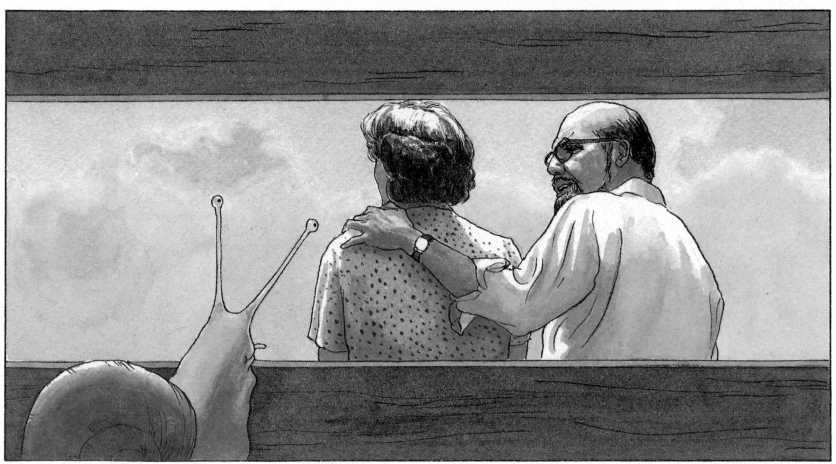

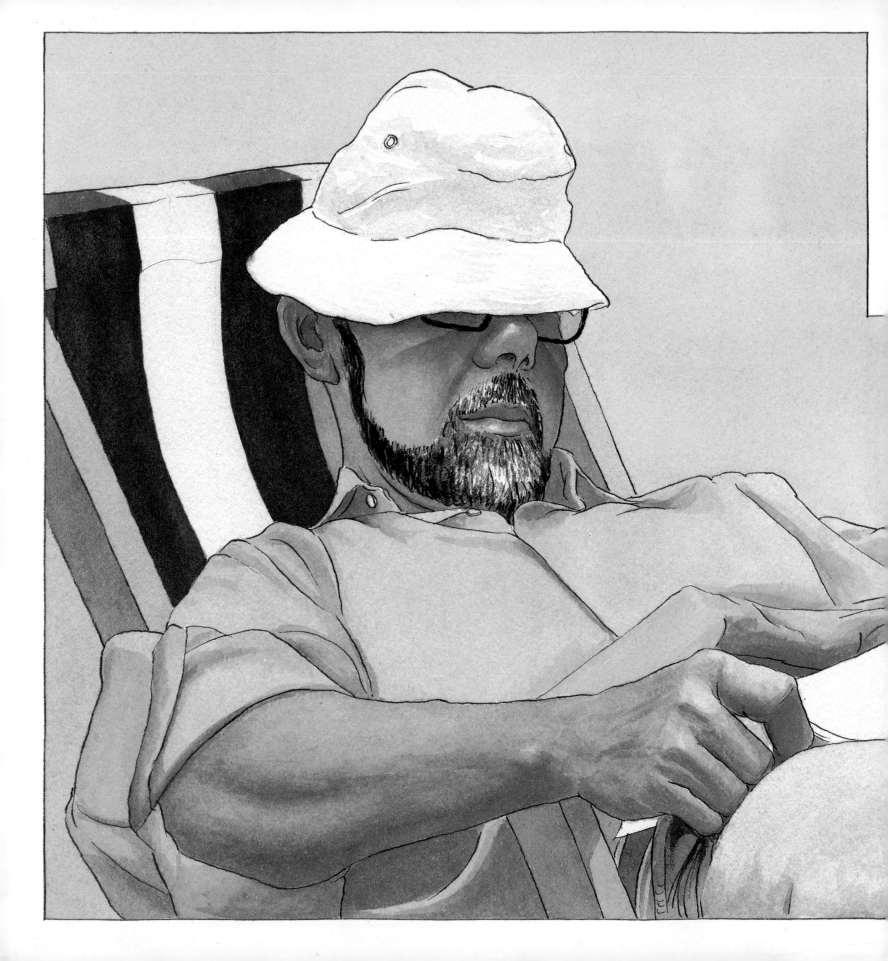

That's when I decided not to read-eat *his* mail anymore.
You don't read a friend's mail, uninvited.
So I didn't nibble that tasty cheque, nor the bill.
I'm the snail who still has a friend.

They were still waiting for that special letter.
On Friday, I ate only TO THE HOUSEHOLDER envelopes.
How boring.
I'm the snail who needs variety.

On Monday, *that* letter arrived from the grandchildren.
Addressed to MR and MRS.
So I didn't nibble.
I'm the snail who just leaves a trail.

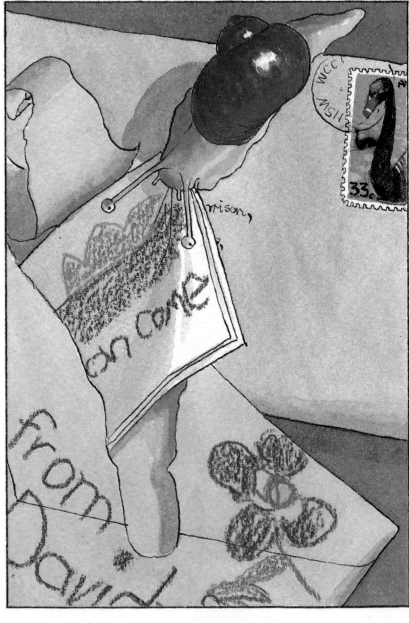

I slithered slowly into *their* car.
Street directories will make a nice change,
while we drive to the farm.
I wonder if I'll enjoy a diet of wheat . . . .

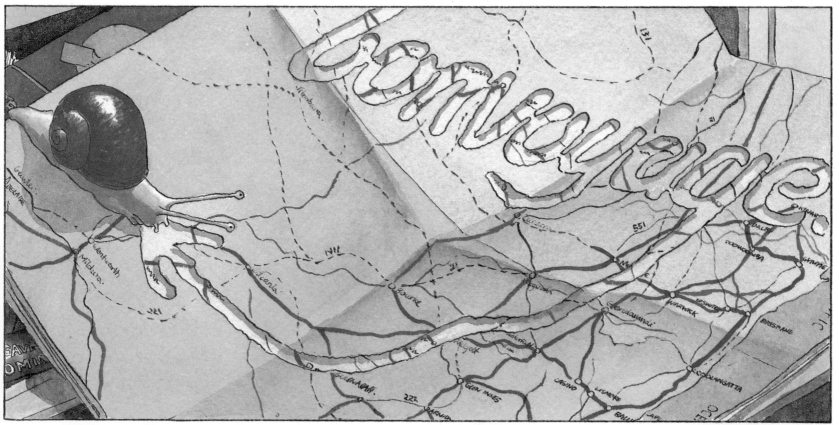